We're Really All Just The Same

by Rod Cornish

Illustrated by
Autumn Wilson

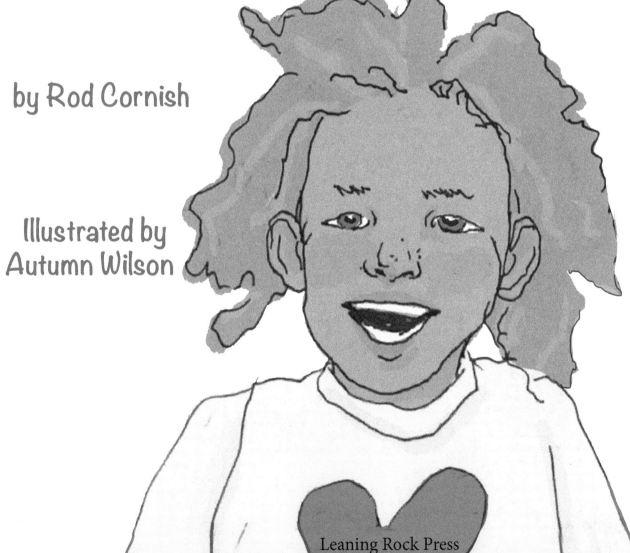

Leaning Rock Press

Leaning Rock Press, LLC
Gales Ferry, CT 06335
leaningrockpress@gmail.com
www.leaningrockpress.com

978-1-950323-56-2, Hardcover

978-1-950323-57-9, Softcover

Library of Congress Control Number: 2021920626

Publisher's Cataloging-In-Publication Data
(Prepared by The Donohue Group, Inc.)

Names: Cornish, Rod, author. | Wilson, Autumn, illustrator.
Title: We're really all just the same / by Rod Cornish ; illustrated by
    Autumn Wilson.
Other Titles: We are really all just the same
Description: Gales Ferry, CT : Leaning Rock Press, [2021] | Interest age
    level: 004-010. | Summary: A book that shows that, despite our
    differences, we are really all just the same.
Identifiers: ISBN 9781950323562 (hardcover) | ISBN 9781950323579
    (softcover)
Subjects: LCSH: Similarity (Psychology)--Juvenile fiction. | Individual
    differences--Juvenile fiction. | Race--Juvenile fiction. |
    Multiculturalism--Juvenile fiction. | Equality--Juvenile fiction. |
    CYAC: Similarity (Psychology)--Fiction. | Individual differences--
    Fiction. | Race--Fiction. | Multiculturalism--Fiction. | Equality--
    Fiction. | LCGFT: Stories in rhyme.
Classification: LCC PZ7.1.C67282 We 2021 | DDC [E]--dc23

Printed in the United States of America

This book was born from a conversation I had with my then four-year-old son, Roen. We were returning from a modeling gig (his, not mine, lol), and I'll never forget. He looked at me and said, "Daddy, your skin is darker, and mine is lighter."

I was thinking, oh man, are we gonna have the race talk already?

Without missing a beat, he looked up at me and said, "It's ok. We're really all just the same."

I was so proud at that moment, and hence the idea for the book was born.

It is dedicated to all the children in the world,
who have ever felt different, who didn't quite fit in.
All of us.
My hope for you is that you discover and love
however uniquely, wonderfully, beautifully different you are
and also realize...

We are really all just the same!

Some kids' skin is black, some white, and some brown.
You'll see every color when you walk around town.
But really each color is just a different name.
We must all remember, we're really all just the same.

We're all good people, want to live and to love.
No need to argue or push or shove.
We all want happiness, no matter what is our name.
Cause deep down inside us, we're really all just the same.

Some kids like flowers, some like horses or bugs.
Some kids like handshakes or kisses or hugs.
Some even like books, tractors, or construction cranes.
None of that matters, we're really all just the same.

Some kids speak Spanish, English, or French.
Some kids are happy to sit reading on a bench.
But as our friend Roen said as he looked up from his game,
"Accept one another, we're really all just the same."

Some kids like grilled cheese, some spaghetti or pie.
Some will eat anything, even if it fell from the sky.
Some like sour lemons, or so they claim.
It doesn't really matter, cause we're really all just the same.

Families can be different, some large and some small. Some kids have a mommy, a daddy, or neither or all. Some have tons of cousins, almost too many to name. Love is what matters, we're really all just the same.

Jane's got blonde hair, and Jack's got dark brown.
The Sullivan twins have the reddest in town.
Whether it's curly or straight, wild or tame,
Our hair may be different, but we're really all just the same.

Some love the beach on a warm, sunny day,
Others stomping in puddles and making it spray.
That's not what's important, sunshine or rain.
Treat people with kindness, cause we're really all just the same.

Some like it cozy and quiet, others like it busy and loud.
Some like being alone, some prefer a big crowd.
We like what we like, there's no need for blame.
When it comes right down to it, we're really all just the same.

Some run like the wind or swim like a fish.
Some can't walk a step but I'm telling ya this:
We're all differently abled, so loudly proclaim.
In some ways we're different, but we're really all just the same.

So you just be you and I'll just be me.
Let's help one another along life's journey.
Remember the tiniest spark can become the mightiest flame.
At the end of the day, we're really all just the same.

22

No one is better than you and no one is worse.
I will say it the last like I said it the first.
Don't let them give you a label or call you a name.
Because deep down inside us, we're really all just the same.

Rod Cornish, Author

Rod Cornish is a native of New London, Connecticut born on May 21, 1965.

He is a father to his son Roen Hendrix, and for the last 15 years has owned and operated a local favorite restaurant, Hot Rod Cafe, known for its award-winning chicken wings and fun atmosphere.

Prior to owning a restaurant and writing this book, Rod's background was almost the complete opposite. Rod earned his Master of Business Administration from The University of Michigan School of Business Administration and went on to work in Finance and Human Resources at several well-known firms in Connecticut, New Jersey, and New York City including General Foods, GE Capital, and Merrill Lynch.

In 2001 after the tragic events of 9/11, Rod decided to take a year off and left the corporate world to travel and learn. He returned from New York City to his hometown of New London, CT, and then traveled for around three months in Europe, mainly Sevilla, Spain. While abroad, the decision was made to not return to the corporate life and to pursue opening a bar/restaurant.

He enrolled in a local adult education program in Culinary Arts at Grasso Tech, where he learned cooking skills and was taken under the wing of Chef Mario Longo who believed in his dream to open his own place. After finishing the program, Rod delved into the business of learning the industry by working for others for several years bartending and working in kitchens and waitering.

Finally, in December of 2005, Rod opened Hot Rod Cafe, which quickly became known for having great wings, beer, and atmosphere. About a year later, Chef Carlos Paucar joined the team and brought the menu up to a new level, winning many awards for Hot Rod Cafe including a trophy in the National Buffalo Wing Competition!

In 2014, Rod became a dad to Roen Hendrix Cornish, the inspiration for this book. A handsome and inquisitive boy who is a perfect combination of his African American Father and Lithuanian Mother.

One day when Roen was four years old, while in New York City for a modeling gig, (Roen modeled from 4 months old to 5 years old when he announced his retirement to his mother and father) Roen made a statement that became the inspiration for this book.

He looked at his father and said, "Dad, your skin is darker and mine is lighter."

Rod thought to himself, "Oh boy, wasn't expecting to have the race conversation this soon."

Then without missing a beat Roen said, "It's ok, we're really the same."

I was so happy and proud of his insight that shortly after that conversation, I began this book. I hope you all enjoy it. We really are all the same and the sooner more folks realize that simple fact, the better off we will all be.

To contact Rod about presentations,

bulk book orders, book readings, or events,

visit his website at:

www.rodcornishauthor.com.

Autumn Wilson, Illustrator

Autumn Wilson is an illustrator and designer based in Southern California. She earned a BFA in Illustration from Syracuse University. You can find her drawing, reading, watching movies…all at the same time.

To see more of Autumn's work,
visit her website at:
www.autumnevewilson.com

CPSIA information can be obtained
at www.ICGtesting.com
Printed in the USA
BVHW020309080222
628328BV00001B/6